Wings

by

James Lovegrove

Illustrated by Ian Miller

First published in 2001 in Great Britain by
Barrington Stoke Ltd, Sandeman House, Trunk's Close,
55 High Street, Edinburgh EH1 1SR

This edition published 2004

ISBN 1-84299-193-0

Printed by Polestar Wheatons Ltd

A Note from the Author – James Lovegrove

When I left university I had no idea what I was going to do with my life. I'd always enjoyed writing stories, so I thought I might try that as a career. My parents were worried, since writing is a risky way to make a living. They said I had a year in which to prove I could do it. Otherwise, I was going to have to get a "proper job".

I wrote my first novel in six weeks. It was accepted by a publisher straight away and was on sale in bookshops within a year's time … just.

Fingers crossed, I still haven't had to get that "proper job" yet.

Contents

Chapter 1

School

The bell rang for the end of lessons. Suddenly the school was filled with moving bodies. The classrooms, library, science room and gym were soon deserted. Lockers and doors were slammed shut, and silence filled the empty rooms. Dust drifted to the floor and settled on scattered sheets of paper.

The children flew through the building with a great racketing roar. Their wings were beating hard. Their screams and whoops and yells celebrated the end of another school day.

They raced along the corridors and down the shafts that led to the main hallway. The corridors, which went sideways, and the shafts, which went up and down, were very broad. They were big enough for four children to fly side by side with their wings fully outstretched.

The children's wings were a beautiful, feathery white. They grew from the children's backs, between their shoulders. Each wing was nearly twice as long from base to tip as its owner was tall.

Streams of children met in the main hallway and quickly filled it. The hallway was very large, but now it seemed too small to contain all these bodies, all this enthusiasm. The school's front doors were flung wide open and the children spilled out into the playground.

Out there in the sunshine, they blinked and stood dazed for a moment, like prisoners who have been released from long sentences in dungeons with no windows.

Then the children started to chat and exchange grins and share jokes. They promised to meet up later that day, or tomorrow, or whenever. They went off in pairs or groups of three or four, with just the odd single one. They rose from the playground with a flap of their wings and flew off along the windy streets of Cloudcap City, with their bags tucked under their arms. The tails of their shirts and the hems of their skirts twirled and fluttered as they scattered in all directions. They looked like the seeds of a dandelion flower, whirled away by a puff of wind.

Meanwhile, still inside the school building, Az plodded along in his usual clumsy manner.

A friend or two patted him on the shoulder and said, "See you, Az," as they flew past him. But Az moved terribly slowly compared with everyone else. No-one could stay beside him for long. It just wasn't possible to fly at such a low speed.

It took Az over a minute to travel the length of a corridor. It took him even longer to climb up or down one of the shafts, using the metal ladders that had been fitted into the walls just for him. It took everyone else a handful of seconds. All the other children swooped like swallows, while Az was a beetle. Like a beetle, he struggled and bumbled and lumbered along.

The last few children were taking off from the playground when Az finally came out into the daylight.

He watched them rise into the sky, wave to one another and flit off. He waved too, in case someone might happen to look back and see him. But it was useless. The children's eyes were fixed on the horizon and home.

Alone, Az trudged across the playground, sunk deep in thought.

Chapter 2
Michael

Normally Az would have caught the air-bus, and travelled home with the old people and the infants. He hated the air-bus. The old people jabbered to each other all the time, and the infants squeaked and squawked and flapped their useless, stubby, little wings. It got on his nerves.

But today, when Az came through the school gates, there was a surprise. His brother Michael was waiting for him on the air-bus landing platform. He was standing beside his gleaming, new Falcon autocopter. Its blades were still spinning lazily.

Michael was watching a pair of girls who were drifting by on the other side of the street. The girls were giving him admiring looks. Michael was a very handsome young man. His wings were so broad and sparkling white that strangers often stopped him in the street and told him how wonderful they were.

Michael forgot all about the girls as soon as he caught sight of Az. He raised a hand and shouted, "Hey there, little brother! Want a lift home?"

Az climbed into the seat beside Michael and dumped his bag between his feet. Michael hit a switch on the control panel of the Falcon. Its blades began to rotate at speed above their heads.

Michael had to yell to make himself heard above the whine of the engine and the *vip-vip-vip* of the blades chopping the air. Michael shouted, "Good day at school?"

Az shrugged his shoulders, "It was OK."

Michael looked carefully at Az. He saw the gloom in his face. It sat there like a raincloud shutting out the light.

Michael didn't ask what the matter was. He just said, "I've got an idea. Why don't we stop by the Ice Cream Palace on the way home? I bet you anything there's a Cloudberry Double-Scoop there with your name on it."

"No, thanks," said Az. He fastened his seat belt.

"Why don't we pop over to the Aerobowl Stadium then?" said Michael. "You know I've got season tickets. Come on. It's a 'friendly'.

The Thunderhead Eagles are playing the Hightown Hawks."

"Oh," said Az.

"*Oh?* What does that mean, *Oh?* The Hawks are playing, Az. You *love* the Hawks. They're your favourite sky-ball team."

"No, it's all right, really," said Az. "Thanks, but I just want to go home."

Michael frowned. "Well, OK. If you say so. If you're sure."

Michael looked in his rear-view mirror and glanced sideways out of the cockpit to check the street was clear. Then he pushed down the joystick. The autocopter lifted from the landing platform and soared into the shining air.

The Falcon was the newest sports model from General Rotors, who were considered to make the best autocopters in Cloudcap City. Michael worked for General Rotors' design department, which meant he had been able to buy the Falcon at a cheap price.

The Falcon was a sleek, tapered machine. It looked like a giant teardrop cast in bronze. Every inch of its bodywork was smooth and gleaming, from nose-cone to tail-fins. Its rotor-blades were so thin that they literally seemed to slice the air.

Michael flew the Falcon in a daring and fearless manner, which was just how it was meant to be flown. He slipped and slid through the air channels. He dipped down suddenly and just as suddenly shot up again. He overtook and undertook the other air traffic. The Falcon responded to every touch on the controls as though it was an extension of Michael's own body and shared his flying skills.

Az ought to have been laughing hard as he and Michael nipped through the other traffic. He ought to have been overjoyed as they whizzed past his school-fellows at top speed, leaving them behind in just the same way that they had left *him* behind earlier.

But today, not even a fast ride in the flash and sporty Falcon could lift Az's depression. If anything, it made it worse.

The autocopter whisked down Sunswept Avenue. The great cubes of the apartment blocks blurred as they sped past. Michael took a right onto Comet Street, then an up into Meteor Road.

Halfway along Meteor Road was the house where Az and his parents lived. Michael had moved out three years ago to a flat in another part of the city. The house had two floors, with a basement below and a big glass dome on top. The windows were large, so as to let in as much sunlight as possible.

On each of the house's six sides there was a huge disc-like magnet. There were magnets like these on all the houses in Cloudcap City. The magnets balanced one another and kept all the buildings in the city afloat in the sky.

Michael brought the Falcon down onto the private landing platform which poked out from their parents' front porch like a tongue.

Az leapt out. He was about to make his way up to the front door when Michael grabbed him by the arm. He turned Az around with a gentle strength, bringing them face to face.

"Listen, little brother," he said softly.

Az looked away.

"I know it's not easy for you," Michael went on. "I know that sometimes it must feel like the whole world's against you, because of what you don't have, or what you *think* you don't have."

Az said nothing.

"Just remember this – it doesn't matter. You're still our Az. Not having one lousy pair of wings isn't going to change that. If I thought it would, I'd cut mine off and give them to you right now. You understand that, don't you?"

Az nodded, not looking up.

"Good," said Michael. "Well, take it easy on yourself. And maybe we'll go down to the Aerobowl Stadium at the weekend. How about that? Would you like that?"

Az nodded again. Michael let him go and was off.

The whine of the autocopter rose behind Az as he wandered slowly up to the porch. Michael yelled out, "See you later!" but Az did not hear him. He had slammed the front door shut behind him.

Chapter 3

Dreaming

"Is that you, Az?" said his mother from the kitchen. She came out into the hallway, drying her hands on a towel. "And was that Michael's voice I heard just now? Is he going to stay for supper?"

Az shook his head. "He's gone off again."

"He's meeting some girl, I expect," said his mother. Lines appeared around her eyes as she smiled.

"Maybe," said Az. "I'm going up to my room."

To reach the upper floor of the house Az had to use a device that his father had built for him. Wooden steps rose through a hole in the ceiling. A similar set of steps went from the upper floor to the dome.

Az's parents used the steps whenever Az was around. As a rule, they walked as much as possible when he was in the house. It was a way of showing respect for their son's feelings since he couldn't fly like everyone else.

Az's room was like any other twelve-year-old's room, except that *his* door went all the way down to the floor. This was another of his father's do-it-yourself adaptations. The carpet was scattered with clothing, books and a jigsaw which Az had long ago given up trying to finish.

There were small model biplanes and autocopters on the shelves. Pride of place went to a scale model of a Falcon which Michael had given Az on his last birthday. Michael had said the model would do until Az was old enough to earn his pilot's licence. Then he would buy him the real thing.

Az dropped his bag into the middle of all the mess on the bedroom floor. He stretched himself out on his bed, lying flat on his back.

He reminded himself that lying flat on his back was the one thing he could do that no-one else could.

That wasn't much of a bonus, though. The other kids at school were *always* asking him to show them how well he could lie on his *back*. Some talent! Some stupid skill *that* was.

He stared up at the ceiling for a long time, trying to think of nothing. At some point during the long, slow fade of the afternoon, he fell asleep.

And he had a vivid dream.

One morning Az wakes up to find he has grown a fully-fledged pair of wings. He doesn't know how they came to be there, he doesn't dare ask why. He simply accepts them.

His parents are happy and amazed. His mother cries. His father rubs an eye, saying there is a piece of grit in it.

Az's parents ask him to forgive them. They do not say what for, but they don't need to. He kisses them both and gets ready to fly off to school just like everyone else, for the first time ever.

Flying, Az finds, is not so difficult. He was born with the instinct for it. Now he has the wings for it. After a little bit of practice, he's on his way.

Heads turn and mouths gape in the school playground. A cry goes up. Look! Look at that! Did you ever ...? Who'd have thought ...? Az is flying!

Az lands in the middle of the school playground and his friends gather round him. They fill the air with excited talk. They fire off a million questions at him. They ask him if they can touch his wings. He tells them they can. They stroke them with wonder and care. It tickles and is rather a nice feeling.

Word gets around, and before he knows it, Az is a celebrity in the school. He is clapped and cheered wherever he goes. There is a hail of hurrahs every time he glides down a shaft with wings outstretched to catch the air. The other children grin and encourage him when he darts along a corridor, keeping pace with them as they hurry from one lesson to the next.

During breaktime Az is asked to join half-a-dozen games of sky-ball. He has never played the game before and has only ever watched from the sidelines. He soon gets the hang of it, however. He even scores a Horizontal Slide.

Az knows he is really popular when Mrs Ragual stops P.E. early and asks him for a demo. The class goes outside, and Az swoops and soars, trying out barrel-rolls and loop-the-loops. Mrs Ragual tells him he is not just a good flyer, he is a brilliant flyer.

Then the other children in the class join him in the air. Under Mrs Ragual's approving eye, they pass a happy half-hour doing what they like to do best, flying stunts. They wheel and whirl and squeal and squall like a flock of mad seagulls. All the time Az is the centre of attention. Everyone is admiring his every move. After all, anyone who can make one of Mrs Ragual's P.E. lessons fun must be a hero.

Az woke up. He was still lying on his back.

Still wingless.

He rolled over onto his side to look out of the window. He saw Cloudcap City, all laid out in neat rows and columns.

The city reached as high as the stratosphere and as low as the tops of the clouds that floated over the Ground as far as the horizon. Tiny, flying figures and aircraft of all shapes and sizes threaded their way along the open spaces and past the buildings.

Most of the buildings were white cubes, but not all. The Freefall Night Club, for instance, was not. It was shaped like a tube. The Aerobowl Stadium was another. It was shaped like a ring doughnut. But the Church of the One True God was the oddest shape of them all. It was a great globe with huge spikes sticking out in all directions.

The air was always clear up here and Az's eyes were sharp. He could make out the trawlers on the cloud-top two kilometres down below. The men on board the trawlers were throwing down their nets into the fluffy, white wilderness beneath them and pulling up flocks of birds. Only some were good to eat, the rest were released to fly again.

He could also make out the immense magnetic towers that ringed the city. They formed the framework which enabled the network of buildings to float.

The magnetic towers looked like tulips. Their tall, slender stems went down through the cloud-top all the way to the Ground. From there they sucked up the raw materials that kept Cloudcap City running. Service lifts crawled up and down the outside of the stems, like tiny insects.

Az lay on his bed looking out at the view for he didn't know how long. Then he heard his mother calling up from the floor below. She was telling him that supper was nearly ready.

Chapter 4
Workshop

Az lumbered down to the kitchen. The smells that were coming from there made his mouth water, in spite of his gloomy mood.

"Go and call your father," said his mother. "Then you can lay the table."

Az went out into the hallway again. He walked a little way along it and stopped at a large trapdoor. The trapdoor led down to his father's workshop. He listened hard and heard faint sounds beneath his feet.

There was banging and tocking, clonking and clanging.

Az's father used to be a maker and mender of clocks, but he had spent much of his spare time trying his hand at do-it-yourself jobs. These were usually for Az's benefit, like all the steps and all the doors in the house.

When he retired from his clock-making, the old man turned his hand to inventing things. He began making a series of useful gadgets. He hoped that one day he could patent them and sell them by the million. They were devices that would make everyone's lives that little bit easier.

So far, not a single one of his gadgets had worked. A portable trouser-press had put the creases in all the wrong places. A clockwork toothbrush had been a gum-mangling disaster. A pair of electric scissors had almost cost him a finger.

But still Az's father went on making these things. He laboured away by the light of a gas lantern, in secret, in strict privacy. Every time he came close to finishing a new invention his hopes rose ... and then that invention would blow a gasket, or slip a cog, or fall apart, or simply fail to start.

Then he would say, "Oh well, back to the drawing board," and heave a weary sigh that was neither a sigh of defeat nor a sigh of despair.

It was almost as if Az's father wasn't really looking forward to the day one of his devices worked. If it was such a success that it made him lots of money, it might mean that he never had to invent anything else again. The old man was happy just to be in his workshop, tinkering, keeping his hands busy and his days filled.

Az called down through the trapdoor. The banging and crashing stopped and his father's muffled voice came up.

"Yes? What is it?"

"Supper," said Az.

"Coming."

A few moments later Az's father bustled into the kitchen. "Give me a hand here, Az," he said and turned round. Az helped him unzip and wriggle his way out of the plastic covers which he wore over his wings to protect them from dust and stray sparks.

Az's father's wings were grey at the edges. They were rough in patches like a young fledgling's wings. They had gaps where the larger feathers had fallen out and would never grow back again. But they were fine, proud wings all the same and Az's mother always used to say they were in excellent condition for a man of his age.

"Outside with those, please," said Az's mother. She pointed at the dusty wing-covers.

Her husband did as he was told and popped the wing-covers out onto the back porch.

"I hate to think what a state that workshop is in," she went on. "Knee-deep in shavings and scrapings and woodchips and what-have-you."

Az's father put his hand over his heart and said, smiling, "I would rather die than have you clean in there."

"I wasn't offering," his wife said. "I was just remarking."

Az's father did not reply at once. He went over to the sink and washed his hands while Az finished laying the table. Then he dried his hands on a towel. As he did so, he said, quietly, as if it was not at all important, "Do you know, I really think I'm onto something this time."

Az's mother had heard her husband say this, or something pretty much like it, a hundred times before. "That's good, dear," she said, without looking up from the stove.

Az said nothing.

But when his father sat down at the table, there was a glint in his eyes Az could not remember seeing there before. They were bright with excitement.

"No, I mean it," he said. "I've been working on a certain project for some weeks now and I think I'm close to cracking it."

"Well, here's your supper," said Az's mother. She set plates laden with food in front of them.

They ate. Az's parents reckoned that their younger son was not in the mood to talk that evening, so they left him alone. They chatted to each other about unimportant things – the events of the day, people they had seen. This is what old married couples do when they relax at the end of the day. They know each other's views on most subjects. All that remains is the nitty-gritty and the splitting of hairs.

Finally Az couldn't wait any longer. "What?" he said.

"*What* what?" said his father.

"What is it, Dad? What are you on to? What's this 'it' that you're close to cracking? What's your new invention?"

Az saw that glint in the old man's eyes again. "Never you mind, Az. Wait and see."

By this time Az's mother was curious, too. "Go on, Gabriel," she said. "Give us a clue."

"What, and ruin the surprise?"

"Is it going to make us rich?" Az asked.

His father made a great show of thinking that question over. "Well, in one sense, yes. In another sense, no." He grinned. He wasn't exactly being helpful. "Wait and see."

Chapter 5

A Mystery

Az waited several days, and still did not know what it was that he would see.

Every afternoon, he would stop quietly by the trapdoor when he got home from school. He would listen to the tink and bonk and clatter and whack-whack-whack coming from below. He would hear his father humming in a tuneless way. His father often hummed like this when he was working.

The sounds seemed no different from the sounds the old man always made down there. They were just ordinary noises. It was frustrating that they gave away no clues.

Several times Az tried to make his father give him some hint of what was taking shape in the workshop, but it was no good. He asked endless questions at the dinner table, and his father always answered with "maybe" or "perhaps" or simply "not saying".

Az remembered that his father had bought several sheets of copper lately. So he asked whether these had something to do with the mystery.

His father replied that he often bought sheets of copper. It was, he said, a very useful and friendly metal to work with.

One evening, Az was flicking through a magazine. He marked off some of the adverts and showed them to his father. "Is it like that?" he asked.

Each time, his father said, "Something like that. Only quite different."

Finally Az got so annoyed that he threw the magazine down and left the room. He heard his father laugh with glee behind him.

Az could not possibly go down to the workshop to see for himself. He did not dare enter his father's most private place. Even his mother was not allowed down there.

So in the end there was nothing for it but to wait and wonder.

One good thing came as a result of the mystery. Az was so busy thinking about what might be in the workshop that he forgot to think about his own problems.

His teachers saw that he was not as gloomy as usual, and they were quietly pleased. They weren't so pleased, though, that he had fallen into the habit of daydreaming in class. Normally he was such a good pupil, and now he was staring out of the window a lot of the time. He paid no attention to what the teachers were saying.

Most of Az's friends and classmates did not notice the change that had come over him. A few of them did notice that Az did not scowl so hard when he walked. His mind seemed to be elsewhere, on something outside himself. They all agreed that this was a healthy sign.

Chapter 6

The Happiest Family Alive

Two weeks after Az's father told the family that he was onto something, he had even more exciting news to announce.

It came one suppertime. Michael had dropped by on his way to pick up a girl called Serena. He was going to take her to a harp concert at the Church of the One True God.

The family were munching their pigeon pie when Az's father tapped his wine glass with his fork. He cleared his throat and said, "A short speech."

Everyone groaned.

"A *very* short speech. Just to say that my new invention will be ready this Saturday. It is going to make us the happiest family alive. I want you to be there, Michael, if you can make it."

"Is this going to be another of your exploding disasters, Dad?" said Michael. "Like the self-heating coffee cup?"

The old man was not going to be provoked. "It's something," he said calmly, "that is going to make us the happiest family alive."

Michael turned to Az. "We're going to be millionaires," he said with a wink.

That night Az hardly slept at all. It was silly, he knew, to get all excited over a dumb invention of his father's. An invention, what's more, that might not even work. But there it was. They had all become infected with the old man's excitement.

And so Az lay awake trying to imagine what form the device would take. He tried to imagine how it could be used, how big it would be, how practical. He ached for Saturday to come.

He would find out then which of the things he imagined, if any, was the right one.

Chapter 7
The Invention

The day arrived. Az and his mother watched while Michael and the old man hauled the new invention up from the workshop and dragged it out onto the landing platform.

The device was covered by a plastic sheet. It was three metres long, thin at either end and bulky in the middle. Az was reminded of the dinosaur skeleton in the Museum of Ground History.

"Well?" said Az's mother. She laughed to hide the fact that she was nervous.

"One moment," said his father. "First, a short speech." As before, the family groaned. This was just what he had planned. So he pretended not to notice. He fluffed out his wings and grasped the edge of his jacket, as if he was speaking at a grand dinner.

"Once," he began, "a thousand years ago, we could not fly. We were not Airborn, we were Groundling. We lived on the Ground. We were limited by the natural boundaries all around us – mountains, rivers, seas.

"But since then, our race has moved onwards and upwards. Now we lead almost perfect lives. There are no boundaries. We can move around freely in every direction in a way that those people long ago would never have thought possible.

"This is the freedom we have won for ourselves. A freedom which we all should share. Every one of us."

Here, he looked hard at Az. Suddenly everyone, except Az, had a pretty good idea what lay hidden beneath the plastic sheet.

The speech might have been longer, but Az's father sensed that he was giving away too much. Like any good showman, he knew he should not let his audience guess what he had in store for them.

He pulled back the plastic sheet with a grand sweep of his arm. The new invention was revealed.

Four faces were reflected in hundreds of small pieces of polished copper. Three of the faces gazed, wide-eyed. The fourth grinned with pride.

Finally, someone spoke. It was Az's mother.

"Wings," she gasped.

Her husband nodded. "Wings," he said.

And wings they were. Larger than life-size, correct in every detail, lovingly crafted in beaten copper.

A pair of metal wings.

Every copper feather was held in place with a small bolt. There were all kinds of joints and hinges to keep the different pieces together. There were balls which revolved inside sockets to allow movement in several directions. A system of wire pulleys and straps connected the wings to a leather harness. The harness was just the right size and shape for the body of a boy of twelve.

"Come on then," said Az's father. He took Az by the shoulder. "Let's try them on, shall we?"

Michael stepped forward to help. Together he and the old man loaded the wings onto Az's back. Then they tightened the straps of the harness around his chest.

Az allowed them to fit the wings on him. He did not know what to think.

The wings were very heavy. When his father and Michael let go, he tottered and swayed. He would have fallen over if Michael had not grabbed him and held him steady.

Az barely listened as his father explained how the wings worked.

"They're designed so that you can use the muscles in your shoulders to make the wings flap. So you should be in complete control. You may have some trouble getting used to them at first, but you'd expect that. Your instinct to fly should take over very soon. Trust me, Az. You'll be up and away in no time."

With Michael and his father on either side of him, Az staggered to the edge of the landing platform. The wings shimmered in the sun and clattered with each step. Hundreds of gleaming, copper feathers rattled against one another.

Az peered down. The uneven surface of the cloud-top seemed awfully far below. The trawlers down there looked as tiny as flies.

He glanced back over his shoulder. At first he could see nothing but copper wing. He dropped his shoulder slightly and the wing flattened out. Now he could see his mother.

There were tears in her eyes.

"Go on," she said to him, smiling bravely. "Don't be scared. You'll be fine."

But Az wasn't scared. He was ashamed. He was clenching his teeth but not because he was trying to be brave. He was trying to hide the fact that he felt even more disabled than ever.

He felt clumsier than ever, weighed down by these huge metal *things*. He felt as if he could neither fly nor walk. He felt like a joke, a parody.

What would they think of him at school when he turned up on Monday morning like this? Strapped into this harness and with these clattering metal wings. "I don't think I can go through with this," Az said. He looked at his parents and Michael with pain in his eyes.

"Don't be silly," said his father. He thought Az's voice was trembling because he was afraid. He did not see that Az was in fact angry. "Michael and I will make sure you're all right. Won't we, Michael? Whatever happens, you won't come to any harm. Trust us."

"Will you at least hold on to me?" Az begged.

"The only way to learn is the way I learned," said Michael. "The way we all learn."

"What way is that?" said Az. There was doubt in his voice.

"The hard way," said Michael. Though his grin was not a mean one, it still made Az feel that he had no-one on his side. He must face this alone.

Michael took hold of Az's arm. Their father did the same on the other side. Together, he and Michael chanted, "One, two, three," and they heaved Az out over the edge of the platform and into space.

And let go of him.

At first, Az couldn't believe what was happening. Then all he could feel was terror as he was swept away in the sickening rush of falling.

The weight of the wings yanked him over onto his back. Down he shot in a clatter of metal. He didn't even try to flap the wings. He was unable even to think about saving himself.

Down he plunged as though in a nightmare, with no thought except that he was going to die. Down he went, past building after building, past windows and doorways, past light aircraft and happy people out for a Saturday-morning glide. Down, down, down, with no hope of being saved.

The platform above him grew smaller. His house and all the houses around it shrank. The sky filled up with more and more city.

Down he fell towards the cloud-top, towards the Ground where his race had come from, long ago.

Chapter 8
Forgiven

There was a soft, nervous knock on Az's bedroom door.

"Can I come in?"

"Sure, Dad."

Az's father entered the room. Az glanced up from the book he was reading, an adventure story about sky pirates.

The old man hung his head. His wings drooped so low their tips were almost touching the floor. The look of shame on his face was so funny that Az could not help smiling.

His father pointed to the edge of the bed. "May I?"

Az nodded.

The old man sat down. There was a long silence while he thought about what he should say next. Then he reached out and laid one hand on Az's leg. He patted the leg in a friendly way but his mind was elsewhere. It was clear that he had several things to say but did not know where to begin.

Az helped him out. "I'm sorry, Dad, if I hurt your feelings."

"*My* feelings?" said his father in surprise.

"By not even trying to fly. By not even giving the wings a chance to work."

"Oh. Well, I wouldn't say my feelings were *hurt*, exactly. I was a little ... disappointed? No, not even that. I did hope ... well, it doesn't matter now. How *I* feel doesn't matter. It's how *you* feel that matters."

"I feel fine. Honestly."

"The doctor said there may be some delayed shock and we should keep you quiet for a bit."

"I feel fine, Dad. I do feel guilty, though."

"Guilty?"

"For letting you down," Az told his father.

"You didn't let me down, Az," was the reply. His father laughed nervously. "How can I get that into your thick skull? I don't mind. Really I don't. I'm just glad that you're alive and well.

"Well, I think I did let you down. I mean, the wings could have worked. I'm almost certain. Of course they would. If I'd tried. I just didn't try. I didn't want to try."

"Oh," said his father. It was what he had been hoping to hear. "Well, anyway, you'll be pleased to learn that I've taken the damn things along to the dump. Never again."

"But you *are* going to carry on with your inventing?"

Az's father frowned. "Perhaps. The fun's gone out of it a little bit."

"But what about making your million?"

"It's just a dream," his father sighed.

"Dreams are important."

"Az," said his father, then paused. "When your mother was pregnant with you, the doctors at the hospital suggested it might be better not to have you. For health reasons.

She wasn't so young any more. But she was ready to take the risk. She was quite sure about that.

"And because she was sure, I was too. We both wanted you more than we'd ever wanted anything. No question about it.

"And when you came, we couldn't have been happier. We loved you the moment we set eyes on you. You were different, but that only made you special."

Az's father looked deep inside himself.

"Even so," he said, "it hasn't always been easy. You understand. Not for any of us. It's the way people look at us sometimes. The pity and sadness in their eyes. It's as if we should be ashamed of something."

He was silent for a few moments. Then he went on, "Anyhow, I was wrong to try and make you the same as everyone else, Az. I thought I was doing something special for you, when of course I was just doing it for myself. And now I can't help agonizing about what would have happened if Michael hadn't gone after you so fast. If he hadn't caught you when he did you might ... you might easily have been killed."

"But he did catch me, and I'm fine," said Az. "I just wasn't meant to have wings, Dad. That's all there is to it."

"Please believe me when I say that I just wanted the best for you. I thought that, assumed that, to fly must be your dream. Your greatest, wildest dream."

"Oh, but it is, Dad. It is. I dream about having wings all the time. But I know in my heart that it is just a dream. The thing is, I've got so used to the fact that it's never going to happen that it doesn't bother me so much any more. Sometimes it's all right to keep a dream that never comes true.

I'd rather have that than accept something that's only second best."

"Say I'm forgiven anyway," said his father.

"You're forgiven anyway."

"Thank you." The old man thought about stroking his son's hair, but checked himself. That was something you did to little children. To boys.

Instead, he patted Az's leg one more time and left the room.

Az shut his book and turned over to look out of the window.

He could see Cloudcap City, his home, spread out in the brilliant midday sunshine. It was huge and bright and busy. The gaps between its buildings were full with traffic, and teeming with life.

It pleased Az to think that, even if only for a handful of seconds, he had dived through that city without help from anyone, without support from anyone. It pleased him to think that he had had a taste of flight, however brief and unwelcome. It filled him with a strange kind of calm.

In this world he would always be different. He would always be wingless. He was stuck forever with walking from place to place. There was no changing that. But in his dreams ...

In his dreams, Az would always be able to fly.

Barrington Stoke would like to thank all its readers for commenting on the manuscript before publication and in particular:

Steven Baton
James Bragg
Simone Daniells
Sophie Evans
Iain Gallacher
Philip Hale-Christofi
Natasha Hartland
Louise Hemmings
Valerie Hirst
Caroline Holden
Russell Johnson
Caroline Loven
Gemma Lucey
Caroline Morris

Bob Parker
Mark Price
Victoria Robson
Esther Ryley
Josh Ryley
Tim Ryley
Helen Sharp
Lorraine Sloggett
Naomi Smith
Daniel Ticehurst
Richard Williams
Faye Willis
Karen Willis

Become a Consultant!

Would you like to give us feedback on our titles before they are published? Contact us at the address below – we'd love to hear from you!

Barrington Stoke, Sandeman House, Trunk's Close,
55 High Street, Edinburgh EH1 1SR
Tel: 0131 557 2020 Fax: 0131 557 6060
E-mail: info@barringtonstoke.co.uk
Website: www.barringtonstoke.co.uk

If you loved this book, why
don't you read ...

Ship of Ghosts

by Nigel Hinton

ISBN 1-842991-92-2

Mick's desperate to go to sea, just
like the dad he never saw. Now he
thinks his dreams are coming true at
last. But his adventures turn into
nightmares as he slowly finds out
about a terrible secret ... what did
happen on the Ship of Ghosts?

You can order *Ship of Ghosts* directly from our
website at **www.barringtonstoke.co.uk**